T0129290

Rusty
the Rat

Rusty the Rat

Rusty Learns To Do It Right
The First Time/Rusty Goes Fishing

VELYN COOPER
ILLUSTRATED BY DONNIE RAY OBINA

Order this book online at www.trafford.com
or email orders@trafford.com

Most Trafford titles are also available at major online book retailers.

Illustrated by Donnie Ray Obina

Printed in the United States of America.

ISBN: 978-1-4669-1133-8 (sc)
ISBN: 978-1-4669-1132-1 (e)

Trafford rev. 10/30/2014

 www.trafford.com

North America & international
toll-free: 1 888 232 4444 (USA & Canada)
fax: 812 355 4082

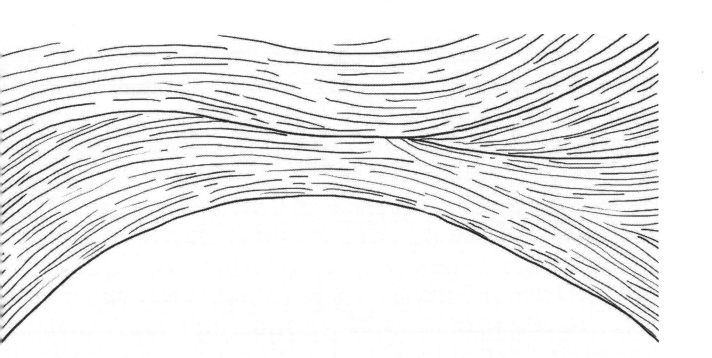

Rusty Learns To Do It Right The First Time

By
Velyn Cooper

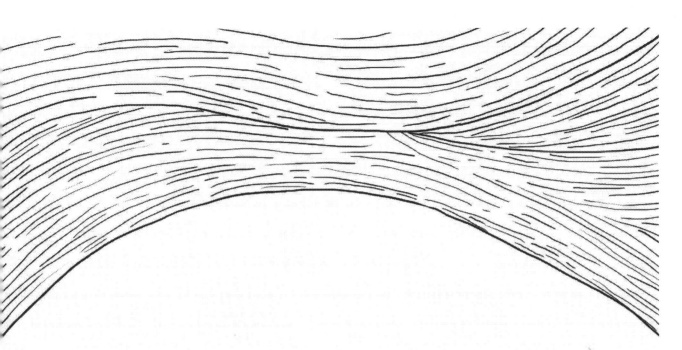

Mother Rat came home tired and hungry after a long, hard day. She had walked for miles and miles in the cold, gathering food for her and Rusty. Now, all she wanted was to feel the warmth of a nice fire, eat supper and curl up in bed for a good night's rest.

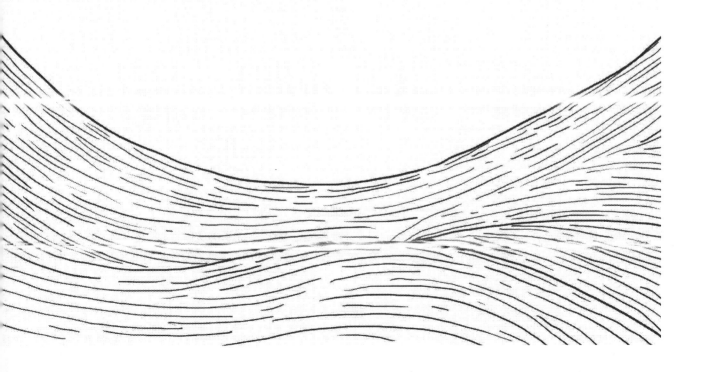

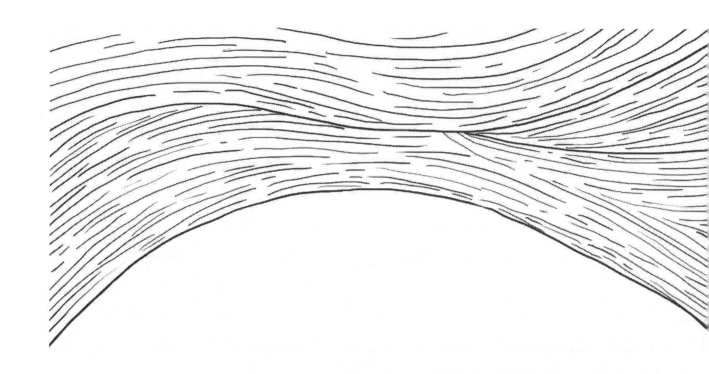

"Rusty dear," she said. "Be a good boy and get some wood for the fire. Make sure and get enough to last until morning because it will be very cold tonight."

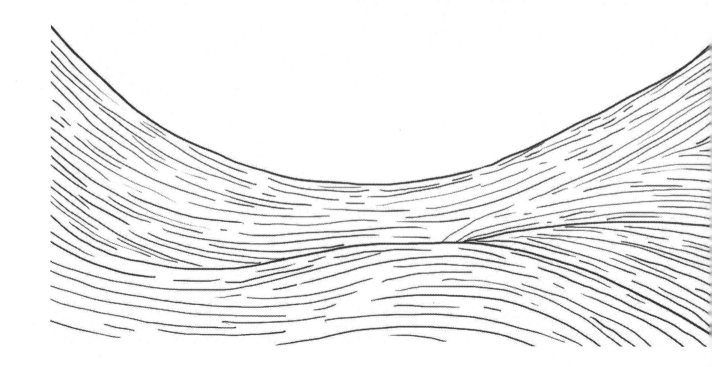

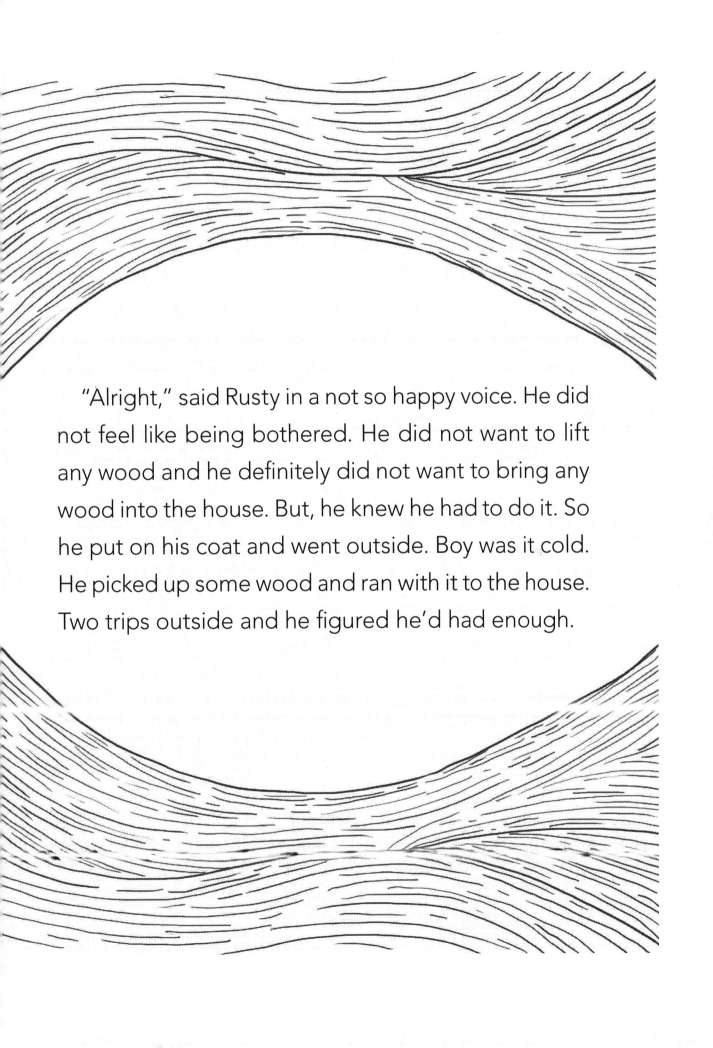

"Alright," said Rusty in a not so happy voice. He did not feel like being bothered. He did not want to lift any wood and he definitely did not want to bring any wood into the house. But, he knew he had to do it. So he put on his coat and went outside. Boy was it cold. He picked up some wood and ran with it to the house. Two trips outside and he figured he'd had enough.

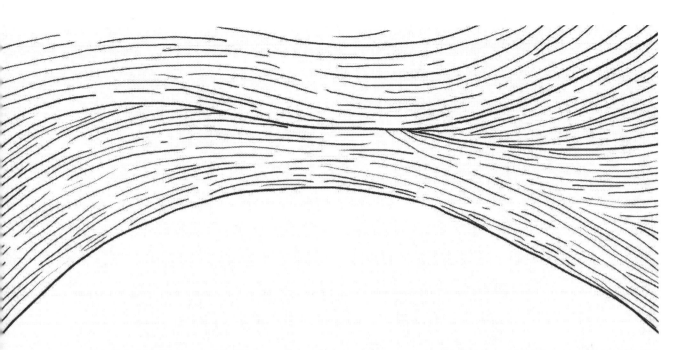

"I am not going out into that cold again," he thought to himself. "This wood will have to do until morning. It will be warmer then and I'll go out and get some more." He knew that the wood was not enough but he had made up his mind—he was not going outside again!

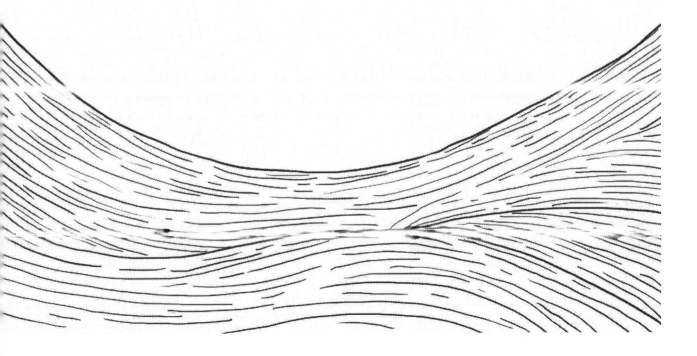

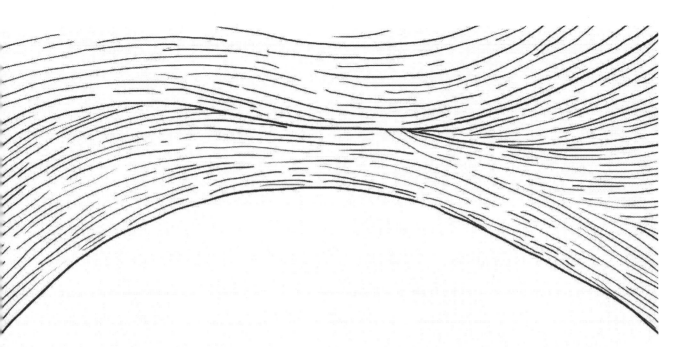

He started a fire and Mother Rat prepared supper. She had gotten a good meal today—chicken, rice and vegetables. It all looked so good and it tasted even better. Rusty ate until his stomach hurt and then he went to bed. Mother Rat stoked the fire and then she went to bed.

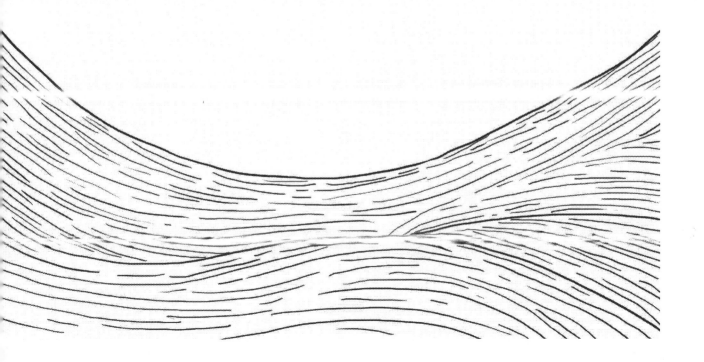

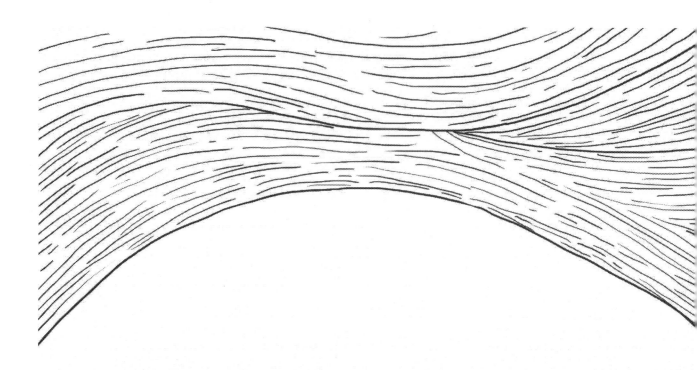

Throughout the night, Mother Rat got up and put fresh wood into the fire—she did not want Rusty to be cold. As the temperature dropped lower and lower and the night got colder and colder, Rusty began to shiver in his bed. He tossed and tossed until finally

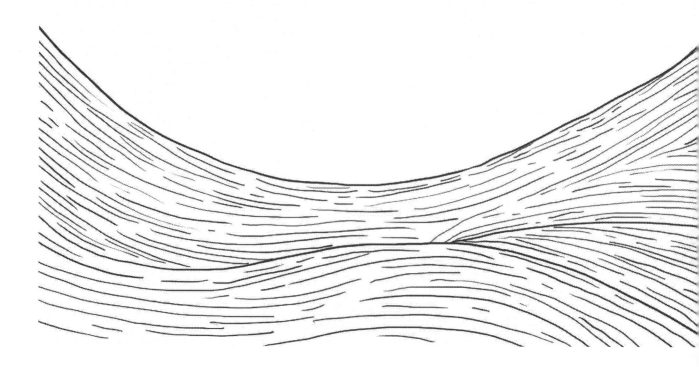

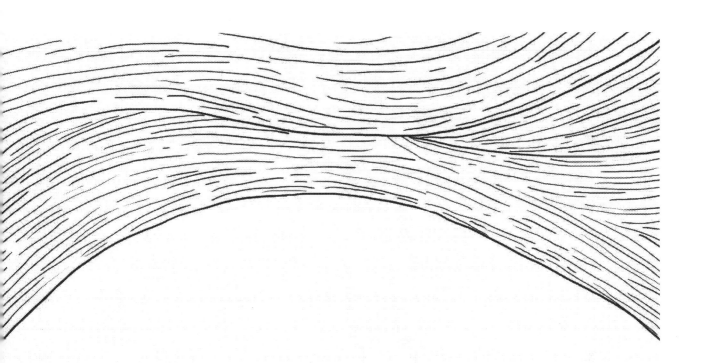

he found a good comfortable position and became warm again. He dared not move now for fear that even the smallest amount of movement would allow cold air to slip under his cover and cause him to freeze.

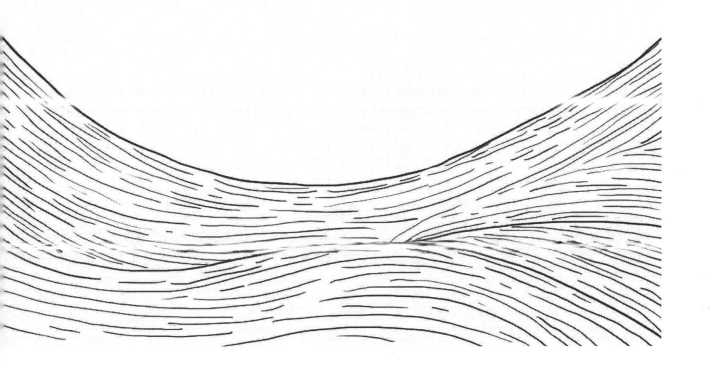

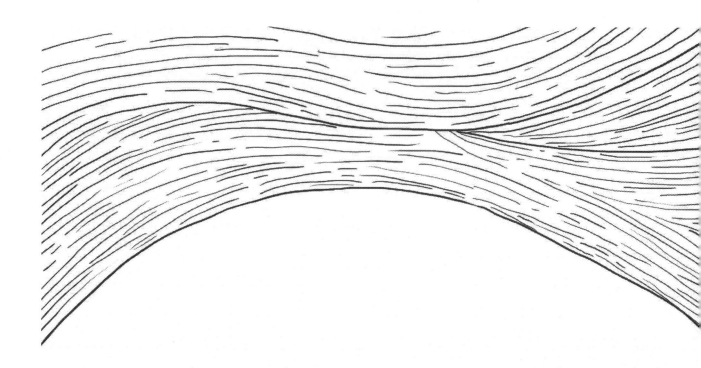

He relaxed his body and was about to doze off into a deep sleep when he heard a shout.

"RUSTY! GET OUT HERE!!"

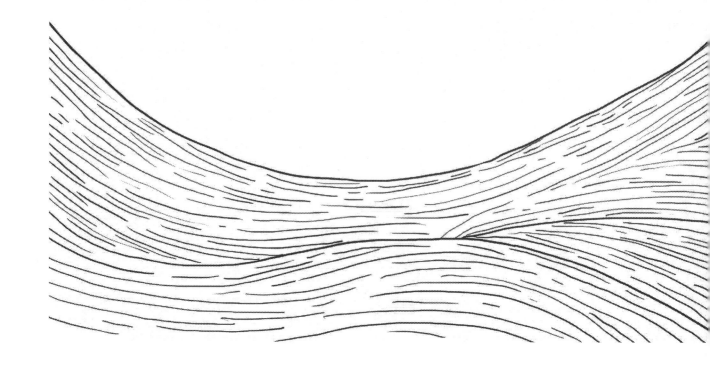

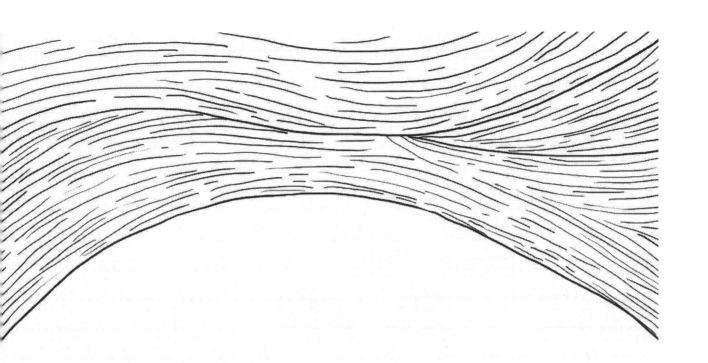

It was Mother Rat and she was mad. There was no more wood for the fire. Rusty jumped out of the bed and dashed into the living room, trembling as he stood before her.

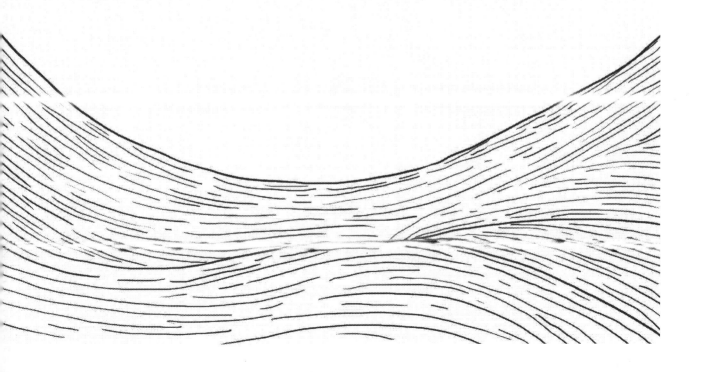

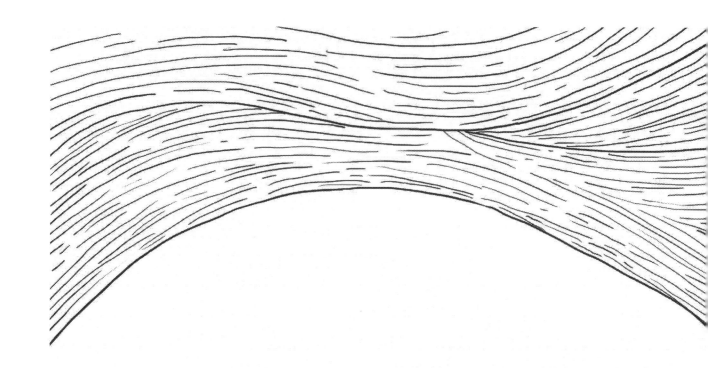

"The fire is dead," said Mother Rat "and there is no more wood. You will have to go outside and bring in some more."

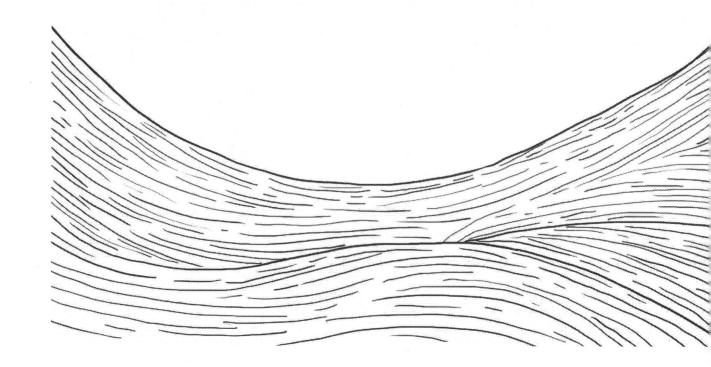

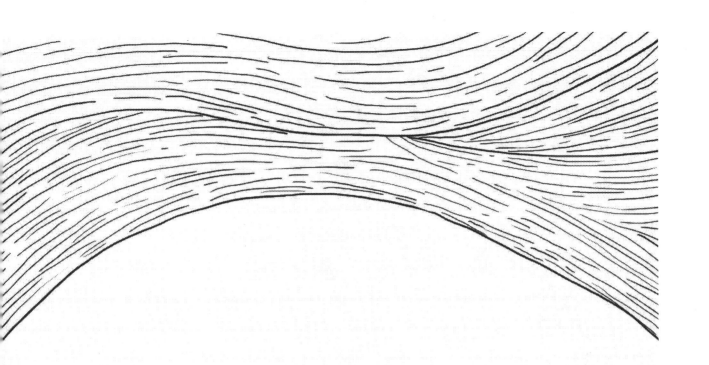

"B . . . B . . . B . . . But," stammered Rusty. "It's so cold. Couldn't you just wrap up real tight in your blanket and lie very still and keep warm?"

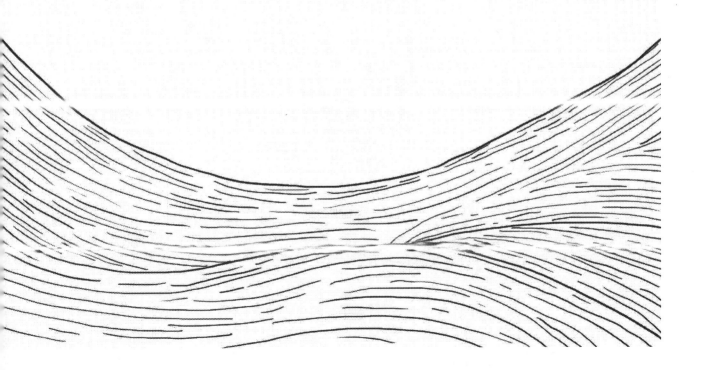

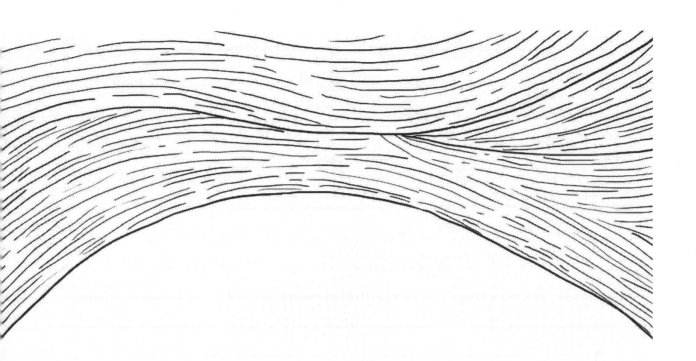

"Yes!" said Mother Rat, raising her voice with each word. "And in the morning they can take us to the toy shop and sell us as stuffed animals because we will be frozen solid! Now go outside and get some wood."

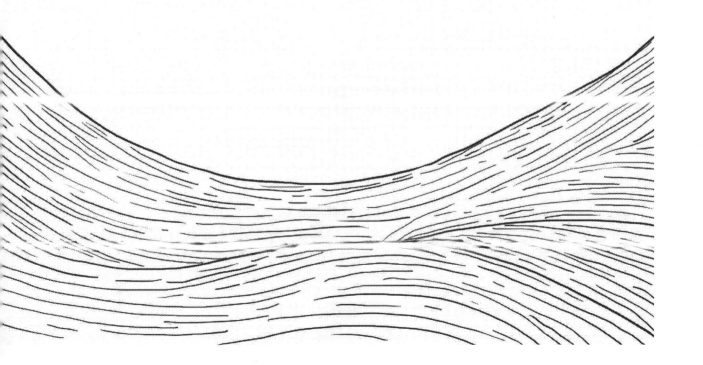

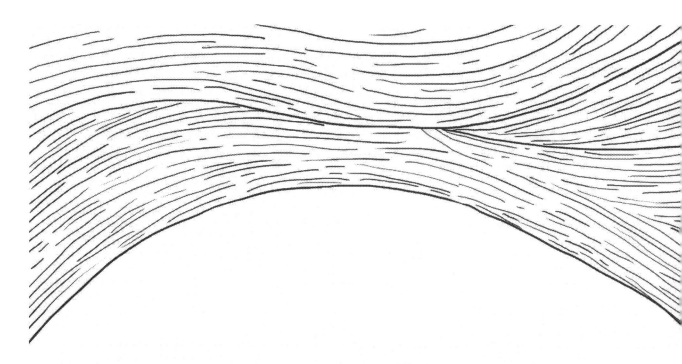

Rusty put on his coat and making each step ever so slowly, he walked towards the door, feeling as if he were going to walk through it for the last time. He placed his hand on the doorknob and opened it just a little bit. He closed it again. It was cooold!

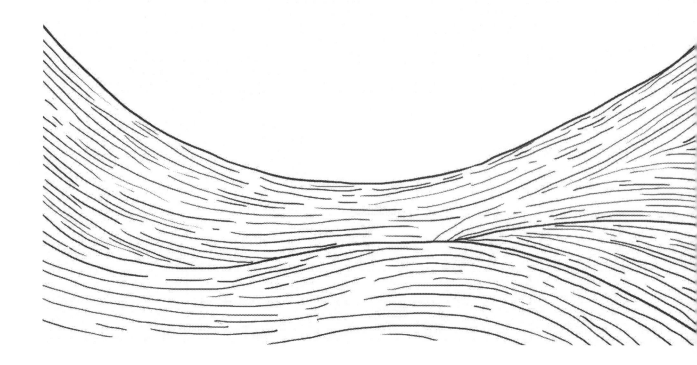

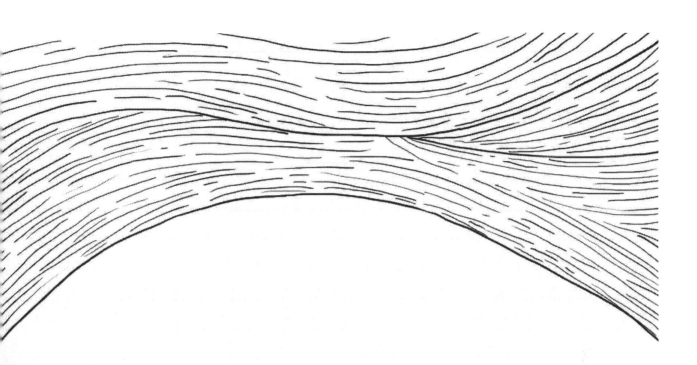

"Rusty" said Mother Rat in a stern voice. He did not wait for her to finish. He opened the door and before you could say "Jack Rabbit," he was outside and then inside again with some wood in his hand. He was shaking from head to toe.

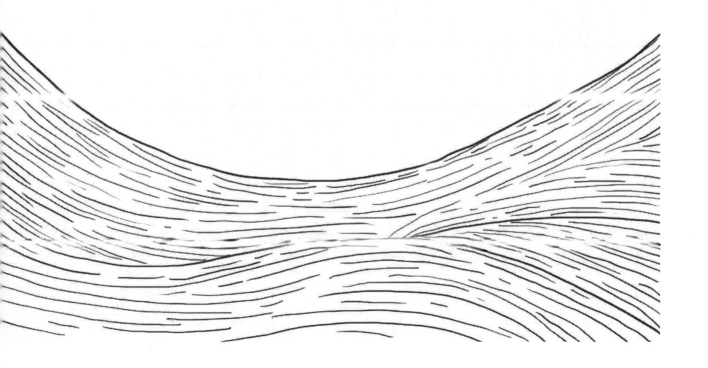

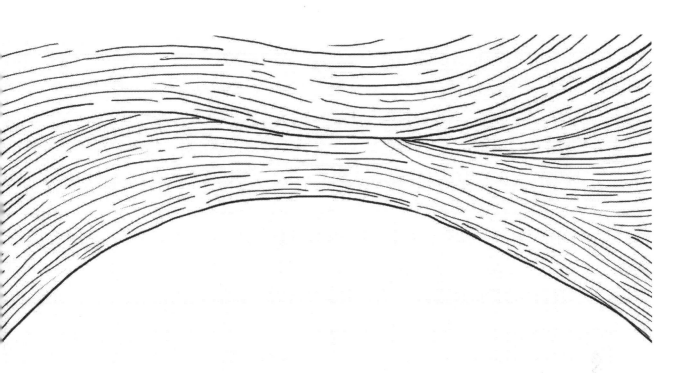

Mother Rat took the wood away from him, started a fire and sat him in front of it. Then she made some hot chocolate for both of them and sat with him.

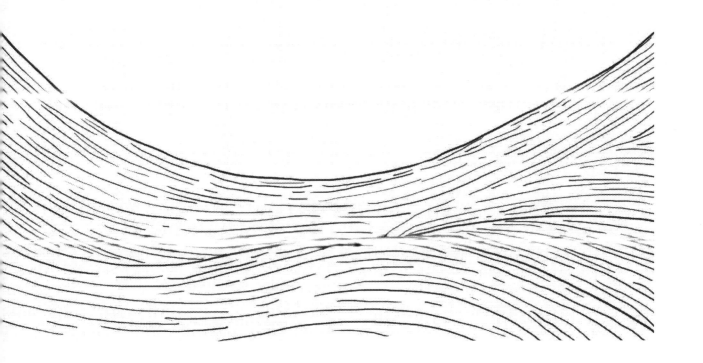

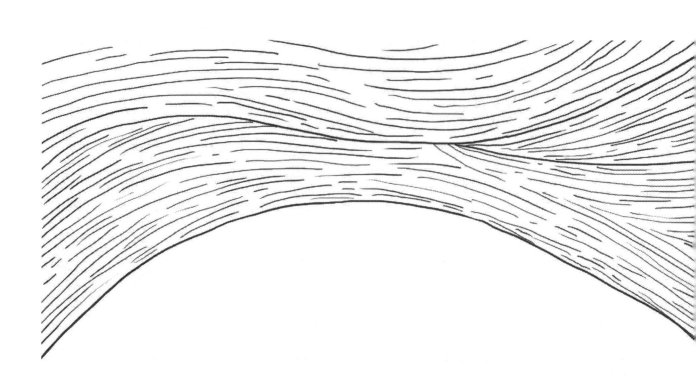

"Now Rusty," she said in a voice full of motherly love. "You knew that was not enough wood to last the night but you chose not to get anymore. If you had only gotten enough the first time, you could have

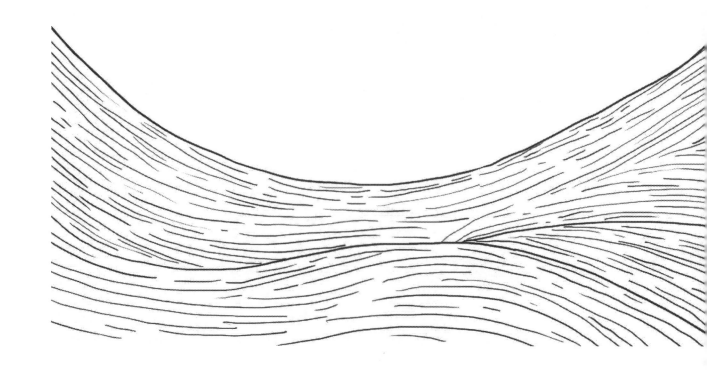

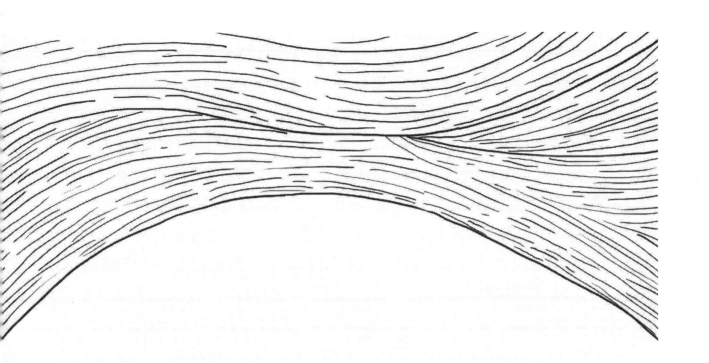

spent a nice warm night in your bed having wonderful dreams, but instead, you had to get up in the middle of the night and face that nasty cold outside. I hope you have learned a good lesson!"

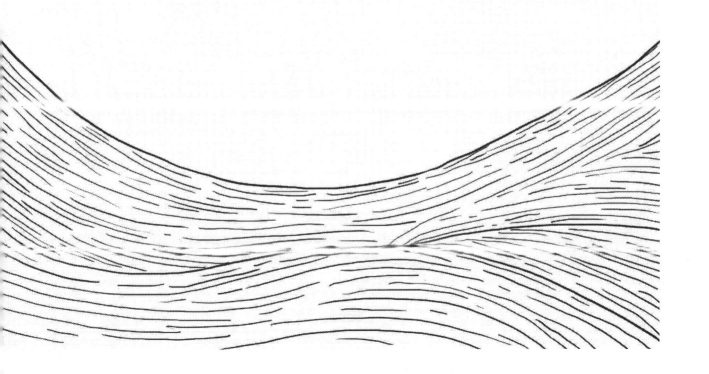

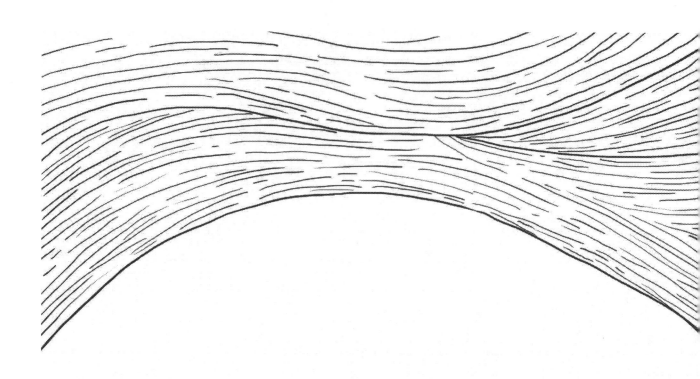

"What lesson?" Asked Rusty.

"Well," answered Mother Rat, "whenever you have something to do—no matter what it is—DO IT RIGHT THE FIRST TIME."

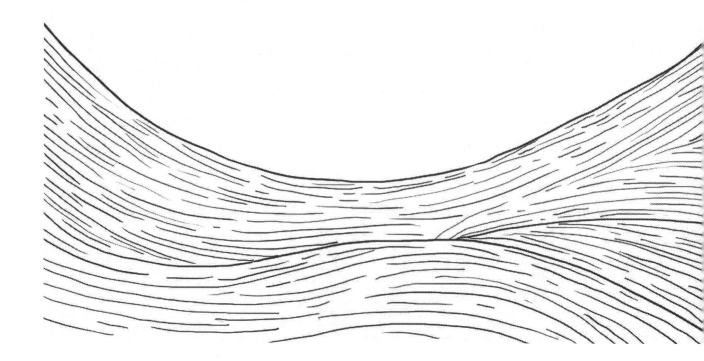

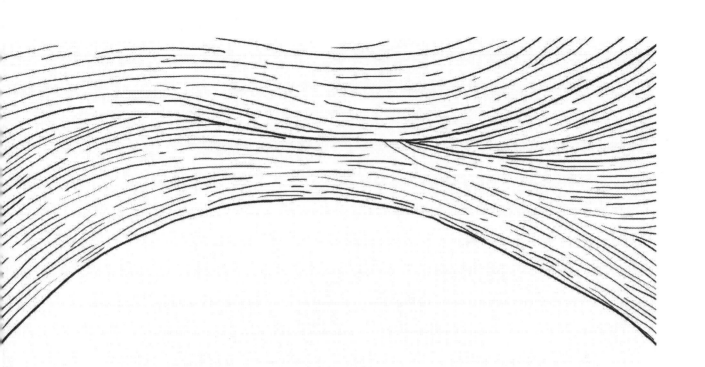

Rusty Goes Fishing

By
Velyn Cooper

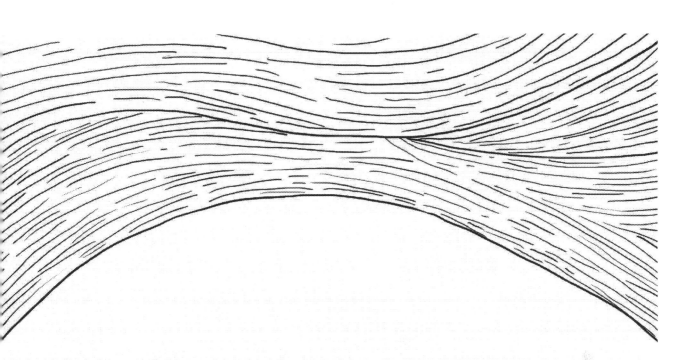

What a beautiful day to go fishing. The sun was shining ever so brightly and there wasn't a cloud in the sky. With his fishing cap on his head, his tackle box in one hand and his lunch box in the next, Rusty was on his way.

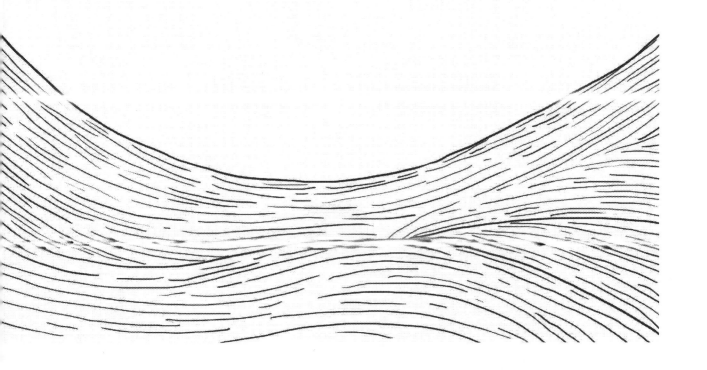

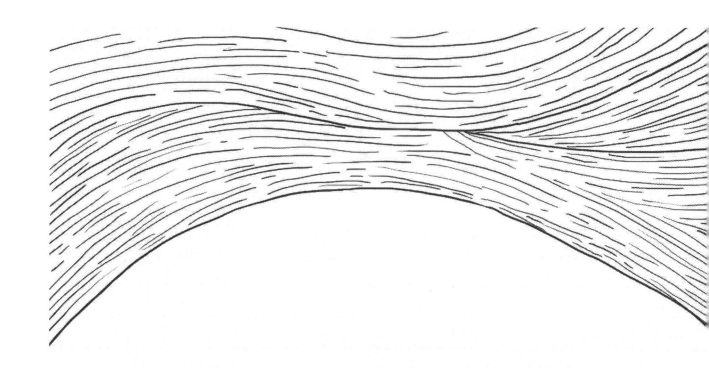

He whistled and hummed and sang as he skipped merrily along to the dock, thinking about the good meal Mother Rat would prepare with the fish he knew he was going to catch.

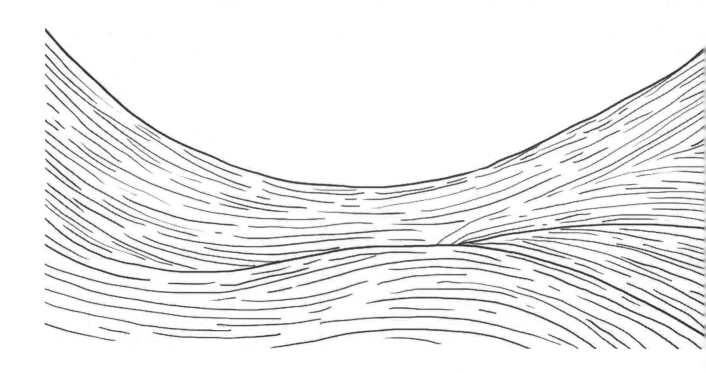

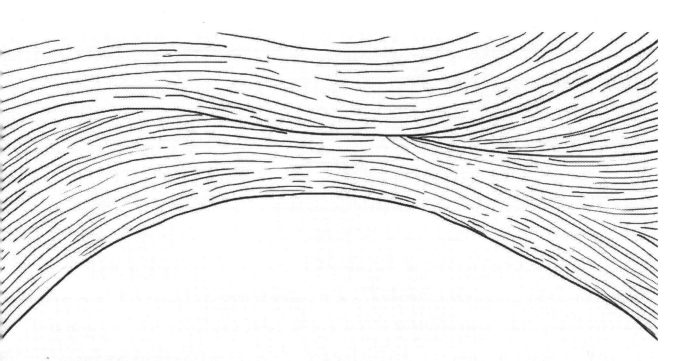

Finally, he was there. He searched until he found a comfortable spot then sat and got ready for the catch. He baited his line, cast it into the water and watched as it disappeared from his sight. After a while, he thought he felt a nibble and gave his line a quick pull, but no, it was just a thought.

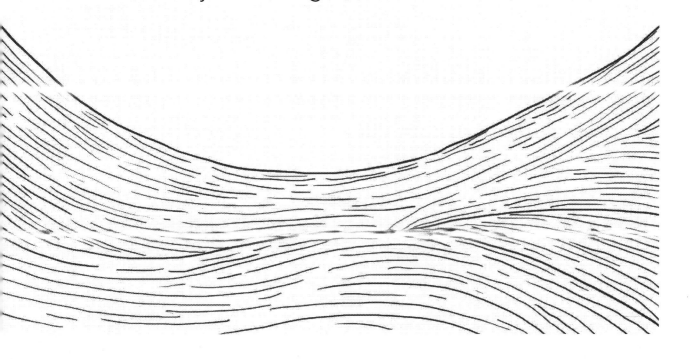

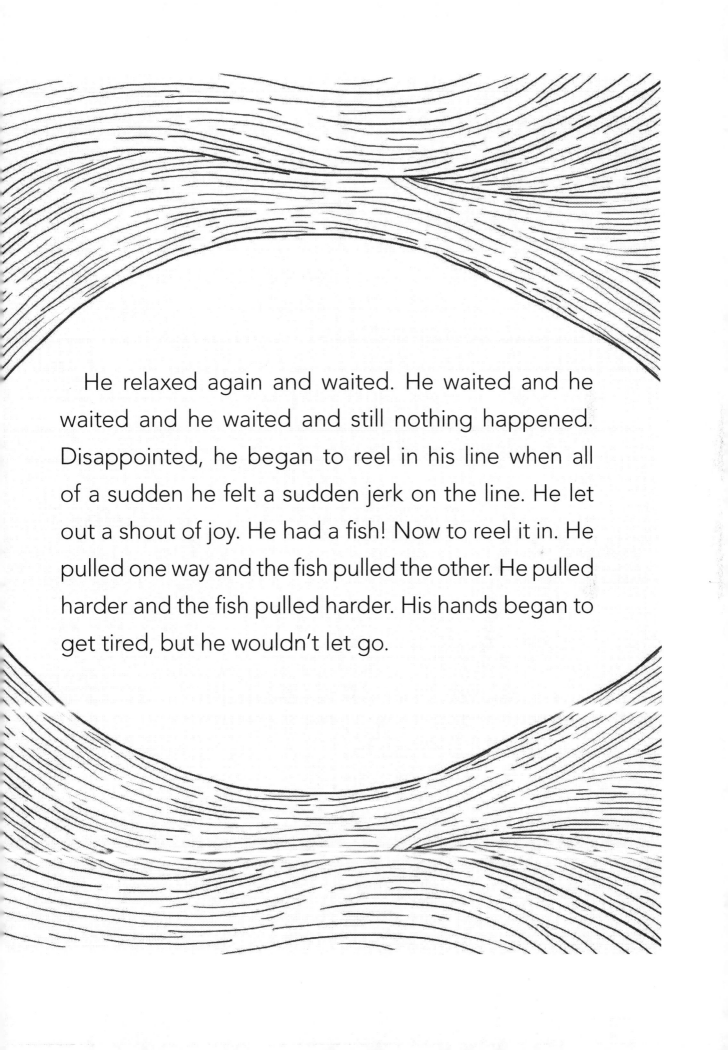

He relaxed again and waited. He waited and he waited and he waited and still nothing happened. Disappointed, he began to reel in his line when all of a sudden he felt a sudden jerk on the line. He let out a shout of joy. He had a fish! Now to reel it in. He pulled one way and the fish pulled the other. He pulled harder and the fish pulled harder. His hands began to get tired, but he wouldn't let go.

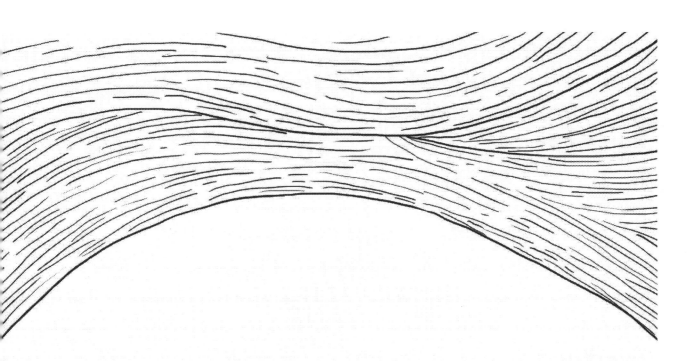

He thought about Mother Rat and how proud she would be to see him come home with a fish that he caught all by himself and he began to pull harder and harder. Like a flash, his eyes lit up and his heart beat

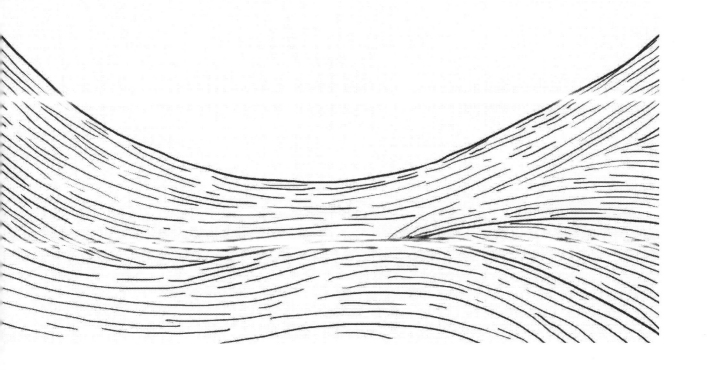

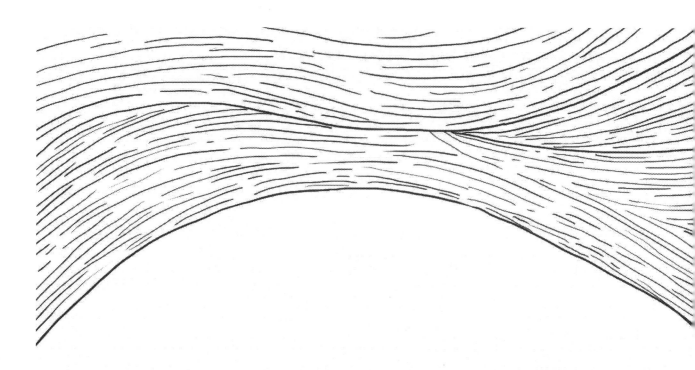

faster and faster. He was excited. He knew that the fish would soon be his. One last pull and there it was—a big, beautiful, shiny fish. He put it on a string and ran home to Mother Rat.

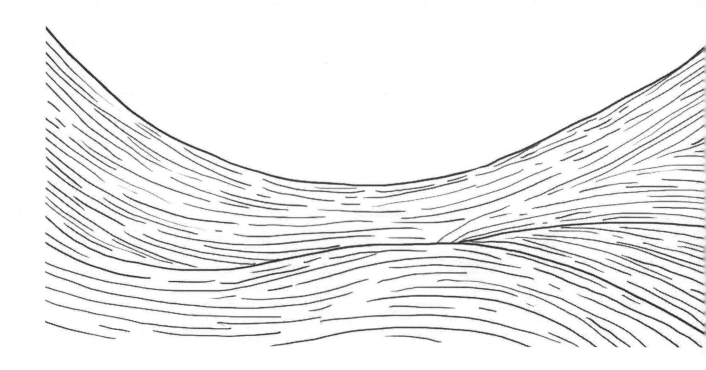

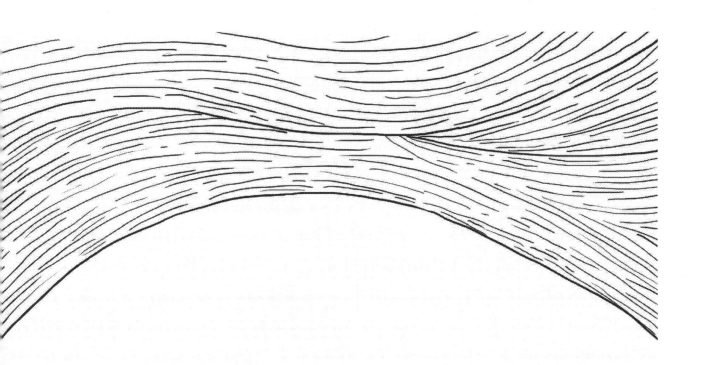

"Oh Mother Rat," he said breathlessly. "I caught a fish. I caught a big beautiful shiny fish. Look at it! Look at it!"

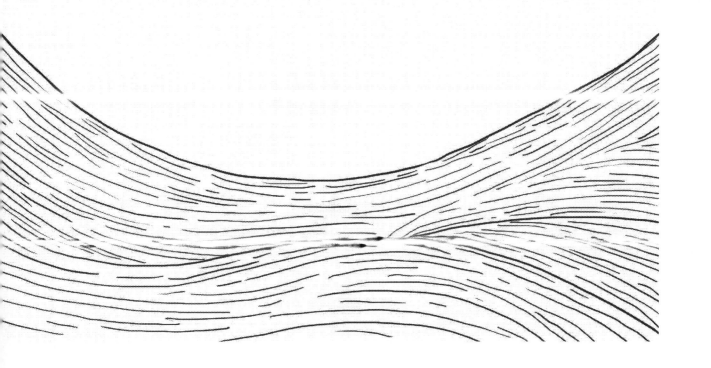

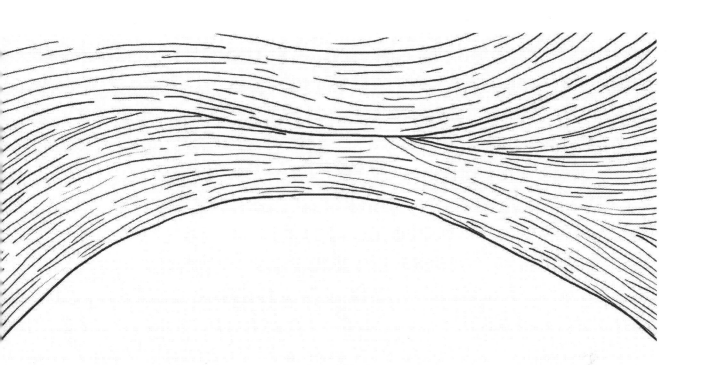

Mother Rat took a look at the fish and lifted Rusty into her arms.

"I am so proud of you, my son. You have done well."

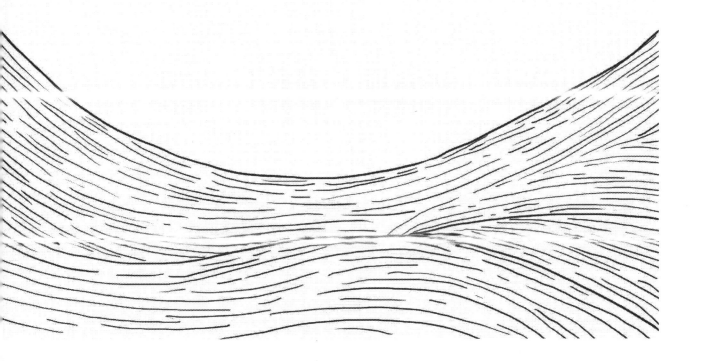

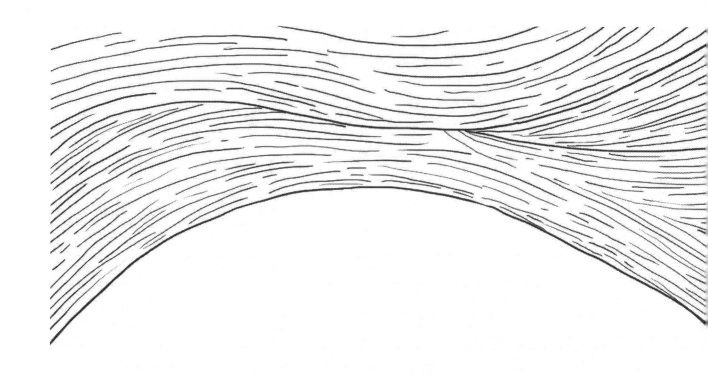

Rusty told her how hard he worked to get the fish out of the water, how his hands ached and how he wanted to give up. Then he told her how he thought

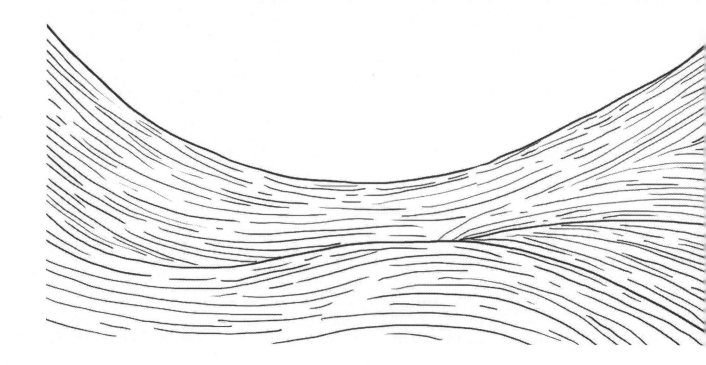

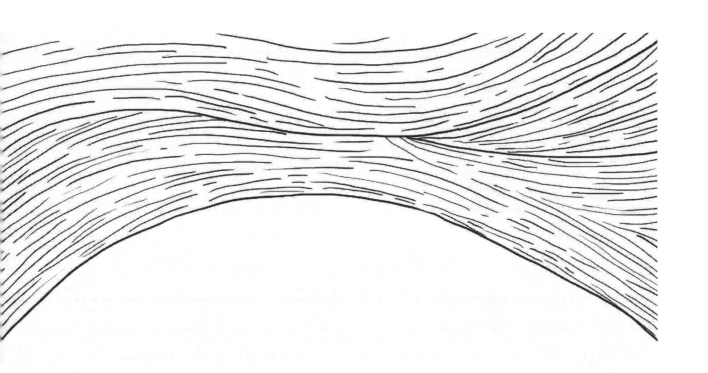

about her and how proud she would be to see him
come home with a fish he caught all by himself, so he
pulled harder and harder until he got his fish.

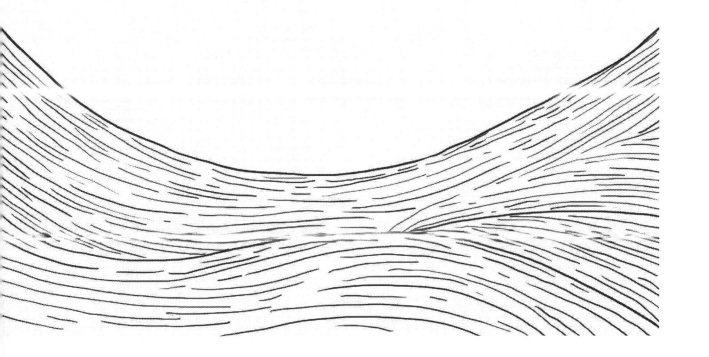

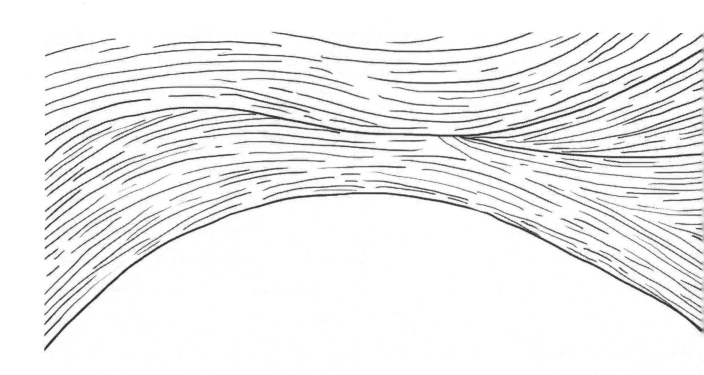

"You know something Rusty," said Mother Rat. "Besides catching your big beautiful fish, you learned a very good lesson—you can do anything you want to, if you try hard enough and never give up."

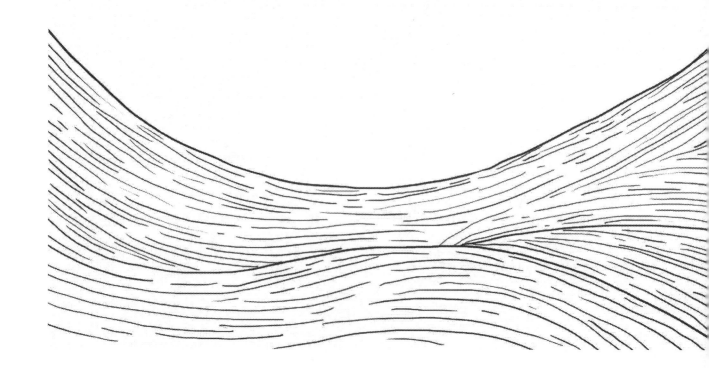

Printed in the United States
By Bookmasters